I0571148

ARCANOCENE

VOL I

MARK M DUNCAN

ISBN: 978-1-7349702-1-0

Cover by Jessica King

For Amy & Jack & Cade & all Allies near and far...

THE ALLIES

Arctodus Divinium — Bill Meadows
Basilocyon — Michael King
Canis No Malus — Joe Paul
Corvus Stellarum — ?!?
Felis Navigatrix — Amy Matthews
Hyenacorvus — Best not to ask
Pteracrotales — As Herself
Smilodon Disrexus — As Himself
Vulpes Oscuria — As Herself
Vulpus Fatalux — As Himself (Screw You!)

SEQUENCE

i	Vulpus Fatalux
ii	Vulpus Fatalux
iii	Vulpus Fatalux
iv	Pteracrotales
v	Vulpus Fatalux
vi	Pteracrotales
s	Corvus Stellarum
si	Canis No Malus
X	Arctodus Divinium
xi	Vulpus Fatalux
xii	Basilocyon
xiii	Pteracrotales
xiv	Felis Navigatrix
xv	Arctodus Divinium
xvi	Vulpes Oscuria
xs	Vulpus Fatalux
xix	Corvus Stellarum
XX	Hyenacorvus
xxi	Vulpes Oscuria

xxii	Felis Navigatrix
xxiii	Vulpus Fatalux
xxiv	Corvus Stellarum
xxv	Arctodus Divinium
xxvi	Canis No Malus
xxsi	Hyenacorvus
xxix	Vulpes Oscuria
XF	Corvus Stellarum &
xfi	Pteracrotales
xfii	Vulpus Fatalux
xfiii	Canis No Malus
xfiiii	Felis Navigatrix
xxxv	Pteracrotales
xxxs	Basilocyon
xxxsi	Vulpes Oscuria
xxxix	Arctodus Divinium
F	Vulpus Fatalux
fi	Pteracrotales
fii	Vulpus Fatalux
fiii	Basilocyon
fiv	Hyenacorvus &

xlvi	Canis No Malus
xls	Vulpus Fatalux &
xlsi	Vulpes Oscuria
xlix	Vulpus Fatalux
L	Felis Navigatrix
li	Vulpus Fatalux
lii	Hyenacorvus
liv	Vulpes Oscuria
lv	Basilocyon &
lvi	Pteracrotales
lvs	Vulpes Oscuria
lvsi	Arctodus Divinium
lvix	Felis Navigatrix
LX	Pteracrotales
lxii	Corvus Stellarum
lxiii	Vulpus Fatalux &
lxiv	Pteracrotales
lxv	Hyenacorvus
lxvi	Vulpes Oscuria
lxs	Vulpus Fatalux

PRELUSION

The crimson lining
Hints of real teeth and hot breath
Our faith is tested

Haikubaritsu

i

S. Disrexus: What is the nature of our existence?

V. Fatalux: What kind of chickenshit question is that?

S. Disrexus: A deep yet meaningful chickenshit question?

V. Fatalux: Beer is better

ii

S. Disrexus: How are quantum mechanics relevant for spiritual insight?

V. Fatalux: Screw you!

S. Disrexus: I had no idea...

iii

S. Disrexus: May I ask a question?

V. Fatalux: May I answer?

S. Disrexus: What is the singlemost advice you have for those who breathe today?

V. Fatalux: Drink good mezcal but don't pay too much. Be nice to tarantulas

S. Disrexus: That's two things

V. Fatalux: Your math is missing some chi, but whatever. Quantities are limited iv

S. Disrexus: What guidance do you have for those who live in this age of Worry?

Pteracrotales: Nothing — I will not grace these master narcissists. They only hear that which pleases them

S. Disrexus: Won't you reconsider? Some will listen

[pause]

S. Disrexus: Why are you looking at me like that!

Pteracrotales: I will not speak to the masses, but I will speak to both of you

S. Disrexus: Both of us?

Pteracrotales: No

S. Disrexus: Both of me?

Pteracrotales: I will address you separately — the one with selective hearing and the one who listens

S. Disrexus: I am listening

Pteracrotales: Liar. But let us proceed —

[pause]

[continued pause]

S. Disrexus: I am ready

Pteracrotales: I have spoken

S. Disrexus: Did I miss it?

Pteracrotales: This venom strips away the unnecessary

V

V. Fatalux: When in doubt, expedite

S. Disrexus: And if it turns out to be a bad call?

V. Fatalux: It won't be your last

S. Disrexus: And if harms those we love?

V. Fatalux: They'll get over it

S. Disrexus: For certain?

V. Fatalux: Don't overestimate your lasting influence

vi

S. Disrexus: I am deluded

Pteracrotales: Yes

S. Disrexus: And afraid

Pteracrotales: Of course

S. Disrexus: My motivations are impure

Pteracrotales: This is unexceptional

S. Disrexus: What then?

Pteracrotales: What would Vulpus Fatalux say?

[hesitation]

S. Disrexus: Too much introspection is the enemy of action

Pteracrotales: Then why do you pretend to ask questions?

S. Disrexus: Because I am deluded and afraid and my motivations are impure

Pteracrotales: And what then?

[pause; projectile vomit via sabercat, including small bones]

Pteracrotales: This took you long enough

S

S. Disrexus: I see you

C. Stellarum:

S. Disrexus: What do you want?

C. Stellarum:

[downpath, briers arc inward from the sides of the trail.
a lichendraped wooden outhouse leans against the great
pine]

S. Disrexus: You're still here

C. Stellarum:

S. Disrexus: Have you anything to say?

C. Stellarum:

S. Disrexus: Then what?

Til when?

The sun is setting. Where did the day go? It's supposed
to be early afternoon, I swear

C. Stellarum:

S. Disrexus: I should turn back. I should go home

C. Stellarum:

S. Disrexus: Why?

C. Stellarum:

[moss wends between the pines]

S. Disrexus: I am tired

[the fallen pine needles are soft. bits of moonlight streak
through those that still wave high]

si

S. Disrexus: Once upon a time it was Friday. Induced delirium settled in like a raccoon that ate the whole pizza

C. No Malus: I had recognized the usual stench before, rising up from misfiring dendritic synapses, like a box of burned out fireworks left in the rain on the 5th of July. This time was different. Worse than ever. It had never happened on a Friday

I felt as if I had been strapped to the Tilt-a-Whirl, force fed funnel cakes, and the drug-head operator had just huffed an 8-ball and shoved the throttle to 'Emulsify'

The Delirium Train left the station. I had a first class, one-way ticket to hallucination hell, spiraling down without a seatbelt

Damn these —

ix

Late afternoon, down at the river: a ripple in low leaves at the wood's edge. A fox snout emerges, sniffs the air, and withdraws back into the green. Moments later a sabertooth cat sticks his head out and likewise sniffs. The sabercat stretches one paw forward and touches the ground but halts and likewise pulls back

Whispers

The other side of the river: a head rises from where the water pools. A darkgray amphibian resembling a 20 footlong salamander lumbers out of the water toward the far wood. It pauses and looks back across the river before it disappears into the low bushes

The fox and the sabercat creep out across the rock riverbank, eyes on the wood past the far shore. The fox's

₃ tails point straight back. A deep chirp issues from the wood. Again and more. They drink quickly, eyes still fixed across the river. They then turn and follow the river south. The chirping goes on for some time after they pass around the bend

The amphibian trudges out of the wood. Water spiders scatter. It slides headfirst into the river, deeper until its tail vanishes. Ripples fade

X

S. Disrexus: Fudge is hard to resist

6 syllables. I must convert to haiku —

Fudge, hard to resist

As in —

Fudge, hard to resist
As a praying mantis moves
Through December's wake

A. Divinium:

Deliciousness persists
Yum
I forgot haiku definition

Because of the word
Fudge

S. Disrexus: Your haikubaritsu defeats mine

A. Divinium: English version of my stomach rumblings

xi

S. Disrexus: How can we spend our time more wisely?

V. Fatalux: The gods

S. Disrexus: I don't understand

V. Fatalux: Show me how you spend your time and I'll reveal your gods

[prolonged silence]

S. Disrexus: I have an uneasy feeling

V. Fatalux: The gods are not perfect

xii

S. Disrexus: I admire you and had intended to seek your view on an issue of substance. But as I framed the question your answer appears likely to be —

'Whichever lives longer'

Is this correct?

Basilocyon: I'm afraid it depends... and even if I'm right, I would still be wrong

S. Disrexus: What if I asked 'when was the last time we slaughtered stuffed pizza together?'

Basilocyon: Sideways is just as tricksy as top down. The answer would still depend... and thinking you can ever know the answer is what leads to the problem. It would be easier to know 'what does everyone want?'

[lengthy pause; moonrise, briefly as orange as sunrise]

S. Disrexus: Time is stronger than cheese

xiii

S. Disrexus: Mistakes were made

Pteracrotales: By you of course

S. Disrexus: Very well. I made this mistake

Pteracrotales: Why is that of concern?

S. Disrexus: It bothers me

Pteracrotales: As it should

S. Disrexus: The results are shackles

Pteracrotales: Is that true?

S. Disrexus: I think so. I don't know

Pteracrotales: Then perhaps you should suffer a while longer

S. Disrexus: But I am tired

Pteracrotales: And Self indulgent

S. Disrexus: You have no compassion. Why should I listen to you?

Pteracrotales: Because I am compassionate

S. Disrexus: I don't know what to say

Pteracrotales: Now you are getting somewhere

xiv

F. Navigatrix: Are you alive?

S. Disrexus: Altered state, navigating the translucent veil between this world and the unseen

F. Navigatrix: Go home

S. Disrexus: Ok. I think I'm doing this wrong anyway

XV

S. Disrexus: I hope you are well today

A. Divinium: Thank you sir, I am better. And yourself?

S. Disrexus: Just attempting to reconcile my flaws with my ideals. Not much going on, really

A. Divinium: Deep stuff for a Tuesday

S. Disrexus: Tuesday? Poxes! Tuesdays are not for introspection. My days are as mixed up as my head

A. Divinium: I put up a marquee in our garden with funky music and flashing lights. Now is the winter of my disco tent

xvi

V. Oscuria: Don't give me that look

S. Disrexus: What look?

V. Oscuria: Don't ask what the look is

S. Disrexus: A hint, if you don't mind?

V. Oscuria: Don't beg for hints

S. Disrexus: I'm not begging, just asking

V. Oscuria: Don't lie, sweetheart. It's unbecoming

S. Disrexus: I am confused

V. Oscuria: Don't blame things on your confusion.

That's shifty

S. Disrexus: How then should I parry the blame, or at least the direction of conversation?

V. Oscuria: Don't change the subject

S. Disrexus: Not without your blessing

V. Oscuria:

On Halloween, rain —
To strengthen autumn's saber,
To water our ghosts

S. Disrexus: —

V. Oscuria: Haikubaritsu

S. Disrexus: I yield

V. Oscuria: This is fun

xs

S. Disrexus: How can we endure when all seems lost?

V. Fatalux: Weylawey! Why did you have to ask that one?

S. Disrexus: It seemed like the right question

V. Fatalux: Now I am melancholy and unable to answer anything. This is your cruelty at work

S. Disrexus: I apologize and retract

V. Fatalux: Now I feel worse. Thank you so very much

S. Disrexus: What can I do?

V. Fatalux: Ask the question

S. Disrexus: The question?

V. Fatalux: Again. Do it

S. Disrexus: How can we—

V. Fatalux: Screw you!

[pause]

V. Fatalux: Better, I win

xsi

Night, a sabercat prowls

Behind, a massive boa glides. They are nearing the lake
where the boa reigns and has dragged his due share of
crocodiles beneath the surface

The sabercat pauses and looks back into the wood. The
boa senses the sabercat's heat, so fetching in this night
compared to the usual crocodiles. Their gazes meet,
only the sabercat doesn't know it. He resumes his prowl

This is how it will happen — the great boa will unfurl
when the sabercat reaches the water's edge. His eyes and
extreme maw will fix the cat's attention until it is quickly
too late — envelopment — the boa will drag him into the
lake and swallow him whole. Tomorrow he will sun his
engorged belly on the shore. This will content him for

some time

The boa has closed half the span between them

Now — the great boa senses that he too is followed. He turns at once — so nimbly for a titan — and beholds a fox. So small, yet how could she have surprised him so? Anger — her rudeness requires payment. Yet she is unstirring as he bears down. Their eyes lock — the boa shakes off a shiver. He releases his jaws and rears back to strike

Then he sees — her left half shows as before — a graceful golden fox. Her right half reveals nothing but unadorned white bones

The strike never happens

The boa sloughs off into the night. Easier prey is somewhere else

xix

S. Disrexus: Hello there

C. Stellarum:

S. Disrexus: Fine, thank you. How are you?

C. Stellarum:

S. Disrexus: Sure, I'd be happy to share my chips. They're a little spicy though

[pause]

S. Disrexus: Well, you don't seem to mind

C. Stellarum:

S. Disrexus: I think I know what you mean. Unless —
wait — you're not referring to mortality are you?

C. Stellarum:

S. Disrexus: Oh. Well that changes things doesn't it?

C. Stellarum:

S. Disrexus: I didn't think this through

XX

S. Disrexus: Something is on my mind

Hyenacorvus: That's where you went wrong

S. Disrexus: It is bothersome, but how should I know what it is?

Hyenacorvus: Start with a bag of char from a campfire pit — add a 2 dollar bill and shake — then add cilantro and do the hokey pokey

S. Disrexus: What will this accomplish?

Hyenacorvus: Huh... that's an interesting question... what are we talking about? I'm thirsty. Hokey pokey

S. Disrexus: —

Hyenacorvus: It's working already!

xxi

S. Disrexus: You are hazardous

V. Oscuria: Why do you say that?

S. Disrexus: I have no claim to insight, but I see that you conceal something ingremantic

V. Oscuria: You are too serious. Has nothing of that other fox rubbed off upon you?

S. Disrexus: Quite a bit, actually. I pay better attention now

V. Oscuria: When?

S. Disrexus: Some of the time. To you, certainly

V. Oscuria: And you fear what I shade. I am honored

S. Disrexus: I don't fear it. Just wary

V. Oscuria: Whatever. It's a matter of degree that shifts with your mood. One mezcal and one bourbon, if you please

[pause; bartender]

V. Oscuria: Not so scary now, right?

S. Disrexus: Far scarier

xxii

F. Navigatrix: What's up with you?

S. Disrexus: I am beset on all sides by enemies. It is taking too long to send them back to the realms of suffering from which they came. Can you help?

F. Navigatrix: Tell them I'm bringing a dragon

[offstage: Sun Tzu, 36 Strategems, etc]

S. Disrexus: They fear you more than they fear me

xxiii

S. Disrexus: We are disenchanted with Consumendarum Voracitas.   Materialism?   Distraction by Design? Whatever you call it

V. Fatalux: Of course you are.   By any name it's a nightmare. There are only 3 sane responses, 2 of which are available to you

S. Disrexus: You will elaborate?

V. Fatalux: Manhattans first

[pause; ice rattles in the shaker, not stirred]

V. Fatalux: Now then... all sane responses are predicated on the following truth — the Voracitas or Whatever is the systemized habit of trading freedom for stuff

S. Disrexus: That's a deft strike

V. Fatalux: The first sane response is to reject the trade in its entirety

S. Disrexus: How is this done? Is it possible in a nonmonastic sense?

V. Fatalux: Mostly catatonics. Beyond that, beer-swilling monks

The second sane response is to embrace the trade in its entirety. Enjoy it for all it offers at the cost of one's freedom, for that is the state of these times

S. Disrexus: A happy hoarder then?

V. Fatalux: Who cares? This path is unavailable unless you reverse your disenchantment, which is too much work

S. Disrexus: I'm guessing the third is more nuanced?

V. Fatalux: Bah! That is correct and terribly wrong. The third is a Pareto Stab at 95% reject, 5% embrace

S. Disrexus: So a bit of compromise and moderation?

V. Fatalux: You misuse Pareto. Think of it this way —

100% rejection costs 13 times more than 95% rejection. So the greatest benefit at reasonable cost is at 95% rejection

The remaining 5% is to be joyfully embraced. In other words, 100% of the 5%, not 5% of everything

Done rightly, the joy and pain of the stab will inoculate against the garbage. This is sweeter than the path of full rejection

S. Disrexus: But don't we risk that 5% creating bad habits like abyssus abyssum invocat?

V. Fatalux: Not if there is sufficient joy and pain. Also, make sure your 5% is inexpensive and doesn't take up much space

S. Disrexus: Like the Divine Garage full of muscle cars I've always wanted?

V. Fatalux: Hot Wheels

xxiv

S. Disrexus: What guidance have you for the Lost?
There are many of us these days

C. Stellarum:

S. Disrexus: But if that's the case, how should we
proceed?

C. Stellarum:

S. Disrexus: Perhaps I did not ask correctly. What is the
right path when mired in disclarity?

C. Stellarum:

S. Disrexus: I am more confused now than when we
started

C. Stellarum:

S. Disrexus: I was afraid you would say that. Vulpus Fatalux warned me

C. Stellarum:

S. Disrexus: Oh, I know he likes you. But once we had the following conversation. I reminded him that —

'Not all who wander are lost'

He replied —

'And not all who are lost care to be found'

C. Stellarum:

S. Disrexus: Ug. Have you not one hadron of wisdom that we can now act upon, that can ease us just a little? We are grasping

C. Stellarum:

S. Disrexus: Oh, if you put it that way...

C. Stellarum:

S. Disrexus: Yes of course, this is just the beginning

XXV

S. Disrexus: I am in desperate need of your help

A. Divinium: Indeed?

S. Disrexus: The details are unclear. This is part of the problem, but I am certain you are essential – the whole thing will fall apart without you

A. Divinium: So there are multiple missing puzzle pieces? Jenga towers will normally stand even if one block is removed from the equation

S. Disrexus: Multiple pieces? Uh oh... this is even more dangerous than I thought

A. Divinium: Evidently danger will knock at the back door as well as the front

S. Disrexus: It is possible I've had too much coffee

A. Divinium: Perhaps an aromatherapy candle?

S. Disrexus: That's for a soft landing rather than an off-the-cliff caffeine crash, right?

A. Divinium: Unless the groundhog sees his shadow, then add 3 1/2 weeks. All connected

[time; lengthy nap; others hibernate]

xxvi

S. Disrexus: Canis No Malus, a peculiar thing has happened

C. No Malus: Please enlighten

S. Disrexus: I reviewed the events of the past season with tribal compadres and ruffians, and it is true that we found a load to bitch and whine upon. But we also found ample cause for joy and appreciation. We just had to go deeper for it, more specifically, and remind ourselves to not be such shitheads

'Shithead' being a technical term

C. No Malus: The key is to let go of the solids and keep the head. Our mortal stopover has a natural transition to a state of traveling light. While here, there should be comfort in the fact that no matter how dark things may seem, we are stardust. We are light

You and your compadres are not wrong

XXS

Behind a roadside tavern – a giant bear and a 3-tailed fox crouch behind a dumpster. Inside – Rainy Day Woman plays on the jukebox. The backdoor floodlights are burned dark, but the streetlight shines high enough to catch the dumpster in its haze. The bear raises his head, looks around, and sinks back down

They creep out. The bear sits and watches as the fox puts an ear to the door and fiddles with the knob. The fox pauses and turns his head to glare at the bear, who looks away and clasps his paws together. The fox pulls the door open. Rainy Day Woman is unmuffled until the fox enters and shuts the door behind him. The bear waits

Rainy Day Woman ends, Wanted Man begins. The bear jolts up straight. His muscles quiver, sending waves through his fur. His back paws tap. He rises on his hind legs, a full ten feet tall now. He shakes ; his arms wave ; he jiggles this way and that ; his hips sway and his eyes glaze. Jig, salsa, jive, boogie woogie — they merge together with spinning kicks and pirouettes

The door opens. The fox backs out, dragging a case of beer with his teeth, a rotisserie hen balanced on top. He lets go of the box and turns warily toward the bear. The fox hisses ; he waves his paws ; he picks up the hen and holds it high to get the bear's attention but to no avail. The dance goes on

Now a homo perturbiens appears at the door. Shotgun. He and the bear lock gazes, time skids — green leaves evolve to gold and red and brown ; they fall ; the wind is harder ; moonlight throbs ; cold descends, and songs come and go. The fox sits and opens a can of beer

Wanted Man resumes. The shotgun smothers it, and the pellets catch the bear front on. He twitches ; he scratches his chest ; he twirls and shakes his hips. The song returns and the perturbiens tries to scream, but nothing surpasses a Wanted Man. The bear tangos up to the perturbiens and grabs the shotgun and smashes it against the back of the roadhouse. The perturbiens rushes back inside and tries to shut the door, but the bear rips it off its hinges and hurls it over the dumpster. He sticks his head through the doorway and roars

The music stops. A sound of breaking glass. The bear

roars again

Snake Farm begins to play. The bear picks up the hen and the case of beer. He and the fox slip back into the trees behind the dumpster and are gone

xxsi

Hyenacorvus: Hey! Hey you! Watcha doin'?

S. Disrexus: Meditating

Hyenacorvus: Is it hard?

S. Disrexus: Depends

Hyenacorvus: You seem to be trying very hard

S. Disrexus: Distractions make it difficult

Hyenacorvus: I know a great story that will help.
Listen –

Once upon a time I was flying through the forest
minding my own business when I saw a bowl of acorns on

the ground. They looked delicious and I wanted them but no sooner had I touched the ground when a giant wolfman jumped out from behind a tree and grabbed me. He was awful – he stood too tall and one of his hands had a monster hooked claw instead of fingers. Eek! He squeezed me so hard with his regular hand I thought my beak would pop off

'What do you want from me?' I wheezed out

"Lunch' he said

'I am unworthy' I said

"I shall judge that' he said

He carried me through the forest and every time I wiggled he squeezed harder. So I just went limp on him

"Don't die yet' he said

'Too late' I whispered. 'I'm dead'

That made him mad

"Oh no you don't' he said. "You're coming back to life so I can kill you proper'

He set me down and opened my beak and began to breathe into me so I bit the hell out of his snout and he howled and I flew up. He jumped up after me but I made it up a tree but he rammed it so hard it fell over so I flew to a thick oak as old as my grandmother's left eyeball. He climbed after me biting and grabbing and slashing so I got an acorn and spat it at him and it went right in his mouth and must have gone down the wrong way because he choked and fell out of the tree and hit the ground hard. I spat more acorns and took a dump on him and flew off and haven't seen him since. I'm sure he's still out there

This has got to be the best meditation, right?

S. Disrexus: I've known worse

xxix

S. Disrexus: You seem moody

V. Oscuria: Do I? It is possible

S. Disrexus: I will assist if you will allow it

V. Oscuria: Assist me in becoming moodier? Forgive me
if that does not sound utterly delightful

S. Disrexus: You know what I mean, of course

V. Oscuria: Do I? That sounds presumptuous and
aggressive

S. Disrexus: —

V. Oscuria: Gotcha!

S. Disrexus: You confound

Fidgeting spirits
Burning moths of entrancement
They crash in your wake

V. Oscuria: This has helped greatly

XF

S. Disrexus: I am grateful to see you

C. Stellarum:

S. Disrexus: About Vulpes Oscuria — is she to be trusted?

C. Stellarum:

S. Disrexus: I believe so, but I have been deceived before in this line of business. And I don't believe Vulpus Fatalux is objective here

C. Stellarum:

S. Disrexus: That's a thought

[breeze; enter Vulpus Fatalux]

V. Fatalux: This looks to be a jeopardous conversation

S. Disrexus: That depends.   Can we trust Vulpes Oscuria?

V. Fatalux: Of course not, but yes

S. Disrexus: Corvus, you see what I'm talking about?

C. Stellarum:

V. Fatalux: Corvus, I brought your favorite bourbon

[pause]

C. Stellarum:

S. Disrexus: Wait. So now you agree with him? Just like that?

V. Fatalux: Don't take the truth so hard

xfi

Pteracrotales: This is antiwise

S. Disrexus: And rather fun

Pteracrotales: Shortsighted

S. Disrexus: We do not care

Pteracrotales: Consequences

S. Disrexus: We accept them

Pteracrotales: Liar. You fail to observe, therefore you cannot accept

S. Disrexus: We accept this lack of knowledge

Pteracrotales: You have been listening to Vulpus Fatalux. This carries its own risk

S. Disrexus: It's probably worth it

[a forked tongue flickers]

Pteracrotales: I never said otherwise

S. Disrexus: Then why do you dissuade?

Pteracrotales: It is terribly funny how one can see and be blind. This applies to all sides, all surfaces

S. Disrexus: Is it possible that—

Pteracrotales: No questions. Drink of this venom and be whole

xfii

S. Disrexus: Why does my heart hurt?

V. Fatalux: Probably from making an ass of yourself

S. Disrexus: What!?

V. Fatalux: And making stupid mistakes, explicitly

S. Disrexus: What should I do?

V. Fatalux: Stop being an ass and stop making stupid mistakes

S. Disrexus: But you said we will always make stupid mistakes!

V. Fatalux: Who is this We?

S. Disrexus: Will it always hurt?

V. Fatalux: Probably. Pain is very personal

S. Disrexus: What makes it better?

V. Fatalux: Mezcal, Ladies, Chicken

S. Disrexus: Is that all?

V. Fatalux: Gumbo

S. Disrexus: My grandmother made holy gumbo. Sometimes I would eat the leftovers for breakfast with the chicken pie

V. Fatalux: Good. You'll be all right. She's still with you

xfiii

S. Disrexus: Wise one, may I trouble you with a question? Yesterday my head hurt but today it doesn't. Does this relate to dysentery of thought? And if so, how is it that today the dysentery is anti-diminished yet the headache was yesterday and therefore preceding?

C. No Malus: Let me get to my cerebro. Check with all the mutants. Could be the work of El Chupacabra

S. Disrexus: There are villains involved then?

C. No Malus: The mutants say the dysentery is competing with the headaches for your attention. They asked — does the dysentery include excessive wordus regurgitatus?

S. Disrexus: Most certainly. This is worse than I thought

C. No Malus: You've swallowed a horcrux. It will pass

S. Disrexus: That is some relief

C. No Malus: The vacuum draft created as it exits will invert the corpus colosseum and reset your flux capacitor. The dysentery should be reduced to two word sentences. Don't argue with women during the reset period or you'll be stuck in the matrix forever. The septic system will survive. The receptacle may not.

S. Disrexus: This makes complete sense

C. No Malus: Anytime

xfiiii

S. Disrexus: Espresso

F. Navigatrix: Me want

S. Disrexus: Things are less burdensome now

F. Navigatrix: That's well and good, but I don't have any

S. Disrexus: It is curious to consider that espresso contains much of the same stardust that we do, just combined in different ways

F. Navigatrix: I'm getting by with a less epic combination

S. Disrexus: I must liberate you

F. Navigatrix: Please

[shares espresso]

S. Disrexus: This may grant visions

[pause]

F. Navigatrix: Or not, but it's still nice

XXXV

S. Disrexus: You seem preoccupied today

Pteracrotales: You observe. Curious

S. Disrexus: With what?

[rattling tail]

Pteracrotales: Unrequited desire

S. Disrexus: O

Pteracrotales: You had to ask

[awkward pause; butterflies drift away]

S. Disrexus: Vulpus and I are getting a beer later. Care

to join us?

[two different bee species work at neighboring flowers]

Pteracrotales: Yes. Timing is essential

xxxvi

Homo perturbiens, they traverse — guns as silent as
spears. Two hounds scurry with them — noses to the
wending deertrail, they huff and impress all

An orange tabbycat with a black-white banded tail lies in
the fallen leaves. She is unseen, yes, but shall she be made
by the hounds? Shall they pierce her scent through the
autumn? Shall they bite upon the crackle of her
overlong tail twitching in the leaves? Or shall it be the
blacklegged golden fox next to her who is undone?

The hounds pause, and the perturbiens obey. They look
through the wood as if their eyes are paleolithic or lucky.
They are neither. The hounds circle the base of a red
oak and a hole going down, down into quiet. They paw
at the dirt, distracted but inobsessed. The cat has seen a
possum go in and out of that hole, or was it the Queen of

Hearts? Absent now, else the hounds would be maddened with delight

The perturbiens understand and command the hounds to cease. The larger hound raises his head and looks nearward the cat and fox. The fox closes her eyes and yawn; the cat regards the squirrel up in the old hickory. Shall the hound see them clearly now? He sniffs the air. Shall he smell the truth? His partner still has her head in the hole, and a perturbiens slaps her on the rear. The sound jolts the watching hound, who just misses

The cat closes her eyes and conceives the squirrel headlong down the trunk and through the leaves. This is not a question. The squirrel conforms and the hounds howl forth. A hillside doe — her flashing white tail would confess her startled presence if anyone were looking. Hounds and perturbiens hunt and do not see

Cat and fox, they rise and plot a different course. A gun speaks through the wood, and the pair keeps the pace until vanishment

XXXs

S. Disrexus: I need your help

Basilocyon: Say the word, brother

S. Disrexus: Fortune cookie, without the dirty sugars
please

Basilocyon: You have a great adventure ahead of you,
and you might be living in a game designed to kill you

S. Disrexus: That's quite a design issue

Basilocyon: Indeed. Never trust the DM

[groundbirds feed through a light sheen of snow]

xxxsi

V. Oscuria: Once upon a time there was a farmer who was known for the plumpness of his hens

S. Disrexus: Did the fox get into trouble?

V. Oscuria: He did, palpably

[the wind is soft, and the fire is peaceful. embers glow as they have for millions of years]

S. Disrexus: But he made it out all right in the end

[embers pop. smoke disappears into the night air. the pause lingers]

S. Disrexus: He did, yes?

V. Oscuria:

S. Disrexus: Why start the story if you're not going to finish?

V. Oscuria: Who said this was a story?

xxxix

S. Disrexus: Arctodus Divinium, there is this curious thing...

A. Divinium: Though I've longed for nothing more than the sleep of ㄱ ancestors, my stomach is grumbling

S. Disrexus: The past ㄱ nights I have sought an old monstrous dream but failed — the dark has been either dreamless or full of other mind embers in which I lose my intent

[pause]

A. Divinium: Let's get some beer

S. Disrexus: Boone's Strawberry Hill?

A. Divinium: No

[beer run]

A. Divinium: The game's essence changes when one tries too hard

S. Disrexus: Yet, some memories prey upon the day

A. Divinium: There is no safety net in what we call dreams. Swinging from one trapeze to the other brings an excitement that pumps like the heart in freefall

[silence, internal deliberation]

S. Disrexus: That sounds right. I'll bring you back something tasty from the circus

A. Divinium: No Boone's

F

S. Disrexus: Our designs seem to trend complexward, and then more so

V. Fatalux: We make things operose

S. Disrexus: This reminds me that I have forgotten something

V. Fatalux: That could be an improvement

[time; constellations shift]

S. Disrexus: Less but better

V. Fatalux: Damn straight

fi

Pteracrotales: Always, beware all pride

S. Disrexus: I will guard against it

Pteracrotales: That is the problem

S. Disrexus: What?

Pteracrotales: You have proclivities and must therefore guard

S. Disrexus: But aren't we all vulnerable in this way? Do you not state the obvious? And if so, what harm is a little pride if it does no harm?

Pteracrotales: Once I flew up the mountain, and on my way I met a great dark tiger whose fur was a black shawl with white rippling through like spring lightning. His mouth was long and scaled and alluded to a crocodile, and his teeth were a cloud of chaos and pain

'Leave my realm at once,' he said. 'My demand is your pleasure'

'I shall depart by my own will and no one else's. I am passing through, up this mountain to the summit where I shall at last see what I intend.' This was my reply

The tiger leapt into the air and clasped his terrible mouth around me and dragged me to the ground. I beat him with my wings and slapped him with my tail as he shook me like a toy and tore my wings. I spied my death in his gaze

[pause; stillness but for a subtle shiver in her wings]

Pteracrotales: I struck out, and my fangs found the deep in his left eye. He howled and a dust storm rose around us. I took to the air, but my ravaged wings would not carry me skyward; I crashed upon a boulder and rested in woe as he thrashed with my venom slipping through him. He slowed and quieted as I waited for him to die

[ache]

He did not die. He rose and saw through me with his stricken eye and snarled and stalked away

I crawled to the top of the mountain and saw nothing that I intended

S. Disrexus: Shall you ever return to the mountain?

Pteracrotales: Must I guard against it?

fii

V. Fatalux: Why so glum?

S. Disrexus: Pteracrotales has confounded me again

V. Fatalux: She does that sort of thing — she's quite good at it, well practiced. You should hear her and Corvus Stellarum go at it

S. Disrexus: Why should I converse with her if it only deepens my delusions?

V. Fatalux: Deepen your delusions? Don't be a shithead. I never said that and would put those odds at a mere 43%. Besides, it's unlikely to be overly mortal

S. Disrexus: I want to believe

V. Fatalux: Believe? In Titanoboa? In a Riskless Hen? In Kasai Rex or Polybius? From what flesh shall you tear out some shreds of belief with those sabers of yours? I myself have faith in a splash of Uncle Val's over ice cream, and no one shall convince me otherwise

S. Disrexus: Torrent!

V. Fatalux: Her venom is most uncommon

fiii

S. Disrexus: I dreamt the bad tiger was chasing me in a night so dark I could only glimpse his stripes flickering behind me as I bled on the forest floor. Then he was upon me, and we fought in the black of the new moon. He was besting me, but you came to my aid and together we drove him away

Thank you

Basilocyon: Mm? Oh, that's how it starts... the ol dodgy tiger. Of course, you know me. This goes without saying

S. Disrexus: Then we found some lively dames. They seemed nice, but they robbed us as we slept and sold us to the circus

Basilocyon: Ha! And some things should just be forgotten... even in metaphor

S. Disrexus: But we told the ringleader that we knew fire tricks. He commanded us to show him, and we burned a hole in the side of the tent and escaped

Basilocyon: Ah, much better

S. Disrexus: Then we found some other lively dames

Basilocyon: Remember what I said about some things?

S. Disrexus: I know, but we couldn't help it. Yet these ladies were still kind to us last I remember

Basilocyon: What to do when the world of metaphor and simile fails?

[eyes on a point past the horizon]

Basilocyon: I'm hungry. And we have an appointment

S. Disrexus: This kind of disorder is pleasing

fiv

Hyenacorvus: That looks kinda cool... maybe?

S. Disrexus: It certainly is not

Hyenacorvus: Can I help?

S. Disrexus: No

Hyenacorvus: I can get it out

S. Disrexus: Uh... no

Hyenacorvus: Come on, you're not going to just leave it
in there are you?

S. Disrexus: I don't know

Hyenacorvus: It's already getting disgusting

[lengthy pause]

S. Disrexus: Make it quick

[howl]

S. Disrexus: That's not quick!

Hyenacorvus: Hold on, it's kinda stuck...

S. Disrexus: Hurry!

Hyenacorvus: Almost got it...

S. Disrexus: Killer!

Hyenacorvus: Oh shove it

[gruesome sound]

Hyenacorvus: There you go. And wow, it's a lot bigger than I thought... you're welcome... hello?

[blue moon, other celestial events]

[awaken, groan; Vulpus Fatalux present]

V. Fatalux: Did you really let Hyenacorvus conduct

surgery upon you? You're braver than I thought

S. Disrexus: O fortunatos nimium, sua si bona norint, agricolas

V. Fatalux: Shove it. By they way, you've been in a coma for 7 days

S. Disrexus: Only 8? The sun's angle is strange

V. Fatalux: I'm nigh speechless. Disminded even to insult you

S. Disrexus: Given the impermanence of reason should we —

V. Fatalux: Screw you! Anyway, did you dream anything worthwhile?

S. Disrexus: Ladies

V. Fatalux: I'm troubled to say it but the surgery was a success

S. Disrexus: A miracle?

V. Fatalux: Don't strain yourself

xlv

Road, debris —

A bluerusted vw pickup on its side ; a propane camp
stove ; a crushtopped guitar, strings in chaos ; a water
heater laid east-west

A feathered serpent flies low. She lands on the truck and
folds her black wings around herself. She sees more —

A watersoaked stuffed t. rex next to a blue hawaiian
shirt ; deer bones

It is bright and cold. The serpent spreads her wings
again and rises over scattered tires ; diffuse scrap metal ;
a doorless refrigerator ; a faded pink plastic tricycle

There — she drops to the road. From an endless vein of

waterfilled potholes: this one — a pawprint in the mud before it, a statement that a great cat once stood here. She dips her head low to the print and flicks her tongue. She sees a whitestriped black tiger with a scaled snout, as large as the slaughtered cow next to which he stands. The pothole reddens

This is now memory but for the pale scent of blood. She continues her search for the next signature

Not far — she glides back to the road once again — a cowskull tower in the center. Stacked 16 high they face her — 16 bleached relics defy the wind — their whiteness clashes with the rainbow iridescence of her scales. Outnumbered, yet she coils before them. She does not blame the skulls, for this is not their design. She rattles, and the wind whistles through their eye sockets. It is bright and cold

She springs and caresses the topmost skull with her wings and holds an extended moment before driving her fangs through bone. This accomplished, she circles the tower 7 times and settles back on the road. Top to bottom, the tower cracks and flows earthward. Now it is a pile of shards. She coils and watches as the sun drifts

Return flight, low

xlvi

Canis No Malus: 200,000,000,000,000

This is the number of galaxies in the Universe

And there are stars

70% of the Universe is Dark Energy. With everything we know about the Universe, we know virtually nothing about Dark Energy. It is the fabric of the spacetime continuum and a key to unlocking mysteries

The Universe is 13.7 Billion years old. Whatever was before that is a complete mystery

The speed of the expanding Universe from the Big Bang was thought to be slowing. It's not — it's increasing in velocity. No one knows why or to where

S. Disrexus: More, please

Canis No Malus: A Black Hole theoretically exists at the center of every galaxy. The Black Hole at the center of the Milky Way is 4 millions times the mass of our sun. Even light cannot escape its gravitational force. We know absolutely nothing about what happens inside or beyond a Black Hole. We can't get close enough to observe

There is a planet with water 729 trillion miles from earth. This is scientifically productive. But for all we know about the Universe, we know very little, really

Some knowledge will succumb to earth's gravitation. Most of it will burn up during reentry

All this is fascinating and comforting to me

[pause]

S. Disrexus: This allows many concerns to wash away

Canis No Malus: Indeed. The Big Bang is gorgeous

xls

V. Fatalux: It is acceptable to use bourbon for a manhattan. Just consider dry vermouth, a bit sparing

S. Disrexus: That wasn't the question

V. Fatalux: Did you see Pteracrotales today? Her feathers were ruffled

S. Disrexus: Literally or otherwise?

V. Fatalux: Does it make a difference?

S. Disrexus: What garnish, if bourbon?

V. Fatalux: Lemon is fine, probably best. One should avoid cherries regardless of conventional wisdom

S. Disrexus: Do you think she's all right?

V. Fatalux: If not then I doubt we'll learn much. She tends to sulk under these conditions unless she can fang someone

S. Disrexus: I hope she's not in peril. What ratio of vermouth to bourbon?

V. Fatalux: Personal preference. Varies with the bourbon, doesn't have to be perfect

S. Disrexus: We should cheer her up

V. Fatalux: If you like getting fanged. You can also add a dandelion leaf to the garnish. This is unexpected

S. Disrexus: Along with the lemon?

V. Fatalux: Yes, as a companion. Or instead

S. Disrexus: We must aid her in this time of tribulation

[pause]

V. Fatalux: Ad gloriam

[mission]

[fangs]

xlsi

S. Disrexus: I am bedeviled by looming divisions. The current design invites personal Destruction. The divergent scheme invites the Unknown, which is preferable to me but brings risk to the tribe. The tribe profits in many ways as things stand, and this is integrous. Does my heart mislead? Is my honor confused?

V. Oscuria: The stars — their light is ancient

xlix

V. Fatalux: You're not looking so bad today

S. Disrexus: Thank you. Today is good

V. Fatalux: You know that today is not any better than yesterday, right? You looked like shit yesterday

S. Disrexus: I feel better today, so today is better

V. Fatalux: That's the wrong way to look at it, but whatever

S. Disrexus: Are all your days the same?

V. Fatalux: Of course not. Yesterday I had 2 plump hens. Today I had 1

S. Disrexus: So yesterday was better?

V. Fatalux: Nope. If you bothered to listen to Corvus Stellarum you might understand

S. Disrexus: I have trouble interpreting the Corvus

V. Fatalux: Hah! I have to agree with you there

S. Disrexus: Do you prefer 1 plump hen or 2?

V. Fatalux: 2

S. Disrexus: So would you say that if we limit the scope of inquiry to hens, yesterday was better for you than today?

V. Fatalux: Nope

S. Disrexus: No difference?

V. Fatalux: I didn't say that

S. Disrexus: What was the degree of difference?

V. Fatalux: Yesterday I had 2 plump hens, today 1. Didn't I tell you that already? You're leading me in circles. That's unexpectedly tricky and I approve. With reservations

S. Disrexus: I still don't understand, but whatever

V. Fatalux: Nice

L

S. Disrexus: It seemed like a good idea at the time

F. Navigatrix: You rely too much on your instincts

S. Disrexus: But I had all the angles worked out

F. Navigatrix: Curves are what throw you

S. Disrexus: Yes, there was statistical uncertainty. But it was rather exciting as well

F. Navigatrix: You will tell me, of course

S. Disrexus: Night fell as a weight. We expected the sunset to linger, yet it did not. Our defenses were not in place, and the insects of the night were silent. This of course meant that we could hear every untoward shuffle and scrape in the dark around us. We felt dangerously exposed

F. Navigatrix: You will say what happened next

S. Disrexus: We realized we had forgotten the pizza, so everything went to hell

F. Navigatrix: Mmmm pizza

S. Disrexus: Yes, but at least most of the injuries were minor

F. Navigatrix: Tell me the rest — you are holding back

S. Disrexus: It is not for sensitive ears, but — Canis No Malus went straight for the fried chicken and devoured it. Basilocyon took a defensive position up the old walnut tree and began throwing nuts at everyone. Arctodus Divinium declared that he would defend the beer and thusly swiped at anyone who came near. Corvus Stellarum spoke in his way and was insightful though I don't remember any of it. Vulpus Fatalux declared that he would not work under these conditions and made off with the coconut creme pie. 'So long, suckers!' he called out as he vanished. Pteracrotales took to the air and laughed at us for being so 'unsettled by the truth.' Hyenacorvus thanked her for being so unhelpful, and they busied themselves with insulting each other. Then Basilocyon fell out of the tree and landed on the hot dogs and Canis No Malus, who was wolfing them now that the fried chicken was gone. Everyone else scurried and worried and fled except Vulpes Oscuria. She hopped on my shoulder and whispered that it was all perfect

F. Navigatrix: That's a lot to digest

S. Disrexus: Nice pun

li

V. Fatalux: What's on your mind?

S. Disrexus: Spirit, courage, and reason?

V. Fatalux: Gross. How so?

S. Disrexus: In a fight I cannot win — retreat is not wrong, correct?

V. Fatalux: Correct

S. Disrexus: But if victory is possible yet I retreat due to a lack of spirit — that is wrong, correct?

V. Fatalux: Lack of spirit is unfortunate. The retreat is not necessarily wrong

S. Disrexus: How not necessarily so?

V. Fatalux: If the result is to find a better fight. You will lack spirit if you are in the wrong fight long enough. Then you cannot win unless your opponent is lazy and stupid. Musashi says no biggie on retreating from a situation you cannot win

S. Disrexus: But Musashi is allergic to a lack of spirit

V. Fatalux: Of course. But spirit is to be cultivated. Wishing and waiting for it to bloom is bullshit. Consider whether you are in the right fight, not whether retreat is valid

S. Disrexus: But what if I believe myself to be in the wrong fight because I lack the spirit that even the weakest among us possess? After all — I am the lowest of the low, an undeserving piece of scum unfit to walk this earth let alone breathe in the presence of living things

[pause]

V. Fatalux: I could bite the hell out of you right now and be justified

S. Disrexus: Thank you for helping me purge. Sunlight destroys mold

V. Fatalux: The spirit can be deceived for only so long. End wrong fights quickly either by victory or retreat, then move on

[pause]

S. Disrexus: You did some excellent pontificating

[continued pause]

V. Fatalux: What... did you say?

S. Disrexus: Pontificatus Maximus

V. Fatalux: Knave! You tricked me

S. Disrexus: You really were good

V. Fatalux: I retract it all

S. Disrexus: You cannot retract Musashi

V. Fatalux: Bad cat! How dare you lecture me on Musashi!

S. Disrexus: Consider yourself lightly. Consider the world deeply

V. Fatalux: I can't believe this

S. Disrexus: Earth, Water, Fire, Wind. Void!

V. Fatalux: I'll Void your face you velvet rogue!

S. Disrexus: Let us gather our friends and serve them manhattans

V. Fatalux: Splendid action!

lii

Hyenacorvus: Stop!

S. Disrexus: Stop what?

Hyenacorvus: Stop that pondering!

S. Disrexus: Why?

Hyenacorvus: It's dangerous

S. Disrexus: How so?

Hyenacorvus: You might explode. Now pay attention
to me instead! Did you know that one time I was flying
around minding my own business when it started to rain
and I have standards you know so I flew down under a
bush and minded more of my own business when the bad

tiger the one with all the extra golly teeth came along sniffing the air and he must've smelled my business cause he came right over to my bush and started shredding it and I hollered I'm minding my own business and he said your business is to die today and I said if you don't leave me alone my sabercat pal is gonna get you and he said let him try and he'll share your business and I looked behind him and waved my wing and said hey buddy you can get him anytime now and the bad tiger looked back and I flew up and away and boy that made him mad and he leapt and clawed at me and got one of my tail feathers it was awful but I made it up and took a dump on his head and flew off

Anyway I think he doesn't like you

S. Disrexus: This is a lot to ponder

Hyenacorvus: Stop! I rescued you!

S. Disrexus: I suppose that's true

Hyenacorvus: No rest for heroes

liii

He resembles a raccoon the size of a grizsly bear

As such he leans against the stone wall and watches the wood across. Dusk, insects speak. Also – his friends are late. A full moon rises, orange and present just scaling the treetops. Behind him – the wood from which he just emerged is still

A fawncolored blackspotted crow lands on the wall and sets down an acorn. The grizsly raccoon pops it in his mouth. Crunch. The crow hops up and down, fluttering. The grizsly raccoon strokes his friend's feathers, and the crow wobbles and tumbles off the wall to the other side. The grizsly raccoon looks down and shakes his head. The crow uprights and shivers and flaps back up and lands on his friend's shoulder

Movement — the insects cannot mask it even with the peepers now in chorus — a coyote barrels out of the wood. Darkening, time slows as he races across the open grass toward the wall. Even in the murk they see the coyote's left eye spinning wild in its socket. The crow burps. The grizsly raccoon watches half the coyote and half the wood during this uneven progress

Once upon a time a coyote runs and his eye might fall out

The coyote defeats time at last and skids-tumbles up to the wall. The grizsly raccoon reaches down and scoops him up and over and all three of them accidentally behold the stars above. They stare skyward in a synapse. The grizsly raccoon cradles the coyote like a baby, the crow still shoulder-perched. Venus and Mars are together. The Pleiades are frisky, and Orion's belt is sturdy. This and more

The crow tips off and plops to the ground, still goggling the heavens. The grizsly raccoon falls backward on top of the crow as the coyote slides from his arms. The lively eye pops out and twirls in the grass. Coyote drool. Otherwise — stillness

Muffled caws. The grizsly raccoon sits up and shakes off the stargaze. The spinning eye — he grabs it and pops it back into its socket. He jumps up and snatches coyote and crow and hustles away from the wall to the near wood

Within — they pass deeper as a buzzing like waspwings
erupts in the distance behind

liv

V. Oscuria: You dreamt it

S. Disrexus: I dreamt, yes. But what is 'it'?

V. Oscuria: A waspwinged viperess wounded you in the early dawn. Stiff with her venom, you fled into a cave. There you found a pool of water wherein you saw not yourself but a dark tiger with a scaled snout

S. Disrexus: —

V. Oscuria: You could sense the viperess stalking you from behind as you gazed into your unfamiliar eyes

S. Disrexus: —

V. Oscuria: You turned and pounced and forced her to

the cave floor. You sank your sabers into her, and her life ebbed in your grasp. But she vanished as if she hadn't been there at all

S. Disrexus: —

V. Oscuria: You felt a great pain as a hooked claw ripped into your belly. You looked up and saw a monstrous wolf with a raptorous clawed arm inside of you. He howled, and the echoing din made your blood shake

[lacuna]

V. Oscuria: So far so good?

lv

[daytime; full moon]

S. Disrexus: Bacon is good. Do you agree?

Basilocyon: Unless it's made of plants or metaphors

S. Disrexus: Beer is good. Do you agree?

Basilocyon: This is tangled, but —

[enter Vulpus Fatalux]

V. Fatalux: Did someone say 'Beer'?

Basilocyon: Things go sideways these days

V. Fatalux: Oh! Are we conducting the Affirmations?
Splendid. Let us now begin

S. Disrexus: We've already started

V. Fatalux: Don't worry, friend. I've got this

Basilocyon! Bacon is good. Do you agree?

Basilocyon: Yes

V. Fatalux: Beer is good. Do you agree?

Basilocyon: Yes

V. Fatalux & S. Disrexus: Do you solemnly swear to salute those about to rock?

Basilocyon: Always and without regret

V. Fatalux: Basilocyon! The floor is now open to your declaration, should you choose. You may go on at length, but not without consequence

Basilocyon: Let us rejoice with bacon and beer. And rock

V. Fatalux: Great secrets are obvious, even under oath

S. Disrexus: I had this under control, you know

V. Fatalux: There is no such thing

lvi

Pteracrotales: Consider essence

S. Disrexus: In what way?

Pteracrotales: Never mind

[her feathered wings are oddly silent as she drifts]

Pteracrotales: Consider essence

S. Disrexus: Yes

Pteracrotales: Never mind

[the stillness is worse]

Pteracrotales: Consider essence

S. Disrexus:

[leaves burn somewhere in the distance]

Pteracrotales: Better

1s

V. Oscuria: Do not ask

S. Disrexus: I have no question

V. Oscuria: Liar

S. Disrexus: Well, perhaps 1 or 2, but they are inurgent

V. Oscuria: I am hallucinating

S. Disrexus: Then you don't mind if I ask?

V. Oscuria: I do not mind

S. Disrexus: What do you see when you hallucinate?

[pause; sleet, temperature drops]

V. Oscuria: Sometimes allies, sometimes adversors. Sometimes it is unclear who is which. It might be terrifying if it weren't so ensorcelling

S. Disrexus: What do you see right now?

[pause; focus]

V. Oscuria: Sleet

S. Disrexus: I will hallucinate with you

[allies]

lsi

S. Disrexus: When you sow and sow and sow some more only to realize that it's just Wednesday — that means more sowing, right?

A. Divinium: There is no end to the seed and it must be sown

S. Disrexus: Somcone tried to kill me this morning. I assume that means more sowing. In other words — cheating death does not earn oneself a reprieve from doing the work, correct?

A. Divinium: Fire in the hole!

S. Disrexus: I'm not a morning cat so they've blown their best chance for today

A. Divinium: Stay alive first. Sow second

S. Disrexus: O. Then it's seasonal...

lix

F. Navigatrix: Why do you hesitate?

S. Disrexus: An integrity issue lies therein. It bestows discombobulation

F. Navigatrix: A famous writer once said 'Integrity, Schimegrity'

[pause; this spring is colder than usual]

S. Disrexus: I'm sorry, was that 'Integrity, Schmegrity' or 'Integrity, Schi-megrity'

F. Navigatrix: Schi - me - gri - ty

S. Disrexus: Ok, but what famous writer? Just curious

[4 crows walk slowly in the meadow, picking in the grass for insects]

F. Navigatrix: Give me everything I want

LX

S. Disrexus: I have a question

Pteracrotales: No

S. Disrexus: No to the question or No as the answer?

Pteracrotales: What ruin if I reply?

S. Disrexus: The space between Perceived Reality and True Reality — is that Inherent Mystery?

Pteracrotales: I am reminded of the tiger. When it is cold my wings might remember pain

[hibernus]

lxi

A crow perches on a pine branch. Mountainside, the sun rises

The valleys below seem infinite in number and scale. Giant ferns rise alongside crystal spires as tall as kapoks. Dragonflies as large as eagles hum among them, and the crystals echo their wingbeats // Homo perturbiens raise cities from dust only for others to destroy them. Their din rises, a seething membrane that moves clouds // Feathered serpents sun themselves on stone pyramids overgrown with moss // An open desert extends in all directions like a galaxy of sand

And another // Darkness. Shadow billows and contracts, whole and timeless

The crow watches a friend approaching from below.

The friend creeps low to the ground, pausing once to look back at the valleys beneath him. Perhaps he is intrigued by the swirling dragonflies or confused by the scheming perturbiens. Perhaps he remembers something said by a feathered serpent. Maybe he misses the desert. Regardless: he looks away from them and resumes the climb

Shadow vibrates in the black, and a tendril lashes out and separates from the greater darkness of its valley. It slithers up the mountain, growing longer and fatter as it ascends. Friend, tendril and crow converge

The crow has seen this and more

The friend passes beneath and beyond, still climbing the mountain as the dark flow closes in from below. Above, the friend roars at nothing in particular. Somewhere a star explodes and the crow understands. These things happen

The dark wraps around the pine. A solitary caw – the crow loses distinction and joins into night

lxii

C. Stellarum:

C. Stellarum:

C. Stellarum: !!!

S. Disrexus: I'm sorry, I didn't hear you at first

C. Stellarum:

S. Disrexus: Yes, I agree that's part of the problem

C. Stellarum:

C. Stellarum: !!!

S. Disrexus: I'm sorry, what did you say?

C. Stellarum:

S. Disrexus: Yes, I suppose I do listen better when I'm dreaming

[later — night, sleep]

C. Stellarum: CAW!!!

lxiii

S. Disrexus: Why am I not enough?

V. Fatalux: Not enough of what?

S. Disrexus: You know. Enough...

V. Fatalux: Oh, that. Mostly from asking such shitty questions

Also because life isn't perfect, and therefore it is

You ok?

Well, that knocked you out cold, didn't it?

[enter Hyenacorvus]

Hyenacorvus: Murderer! Why did you kill him?

V. Fatalux: Oh what do you want? And anyway he's not dead

Hyenacorvus: Prepare for Battle!

V. Fatalux: He'll be fine. He just has truth flu

Hyenacorvus: Ohhh... well why didn't you say so? Hey, are those chips? Can I have some?

V. Fatalux: Sure. They're his. Have all you want

[snack]

V. Fatalux: Now that you mention it, I think he'd rather see you than me when he wakes up

Hyenacorvus: I shall stand guard

[exit Vulpus Fatalux; time passes; a well deserved nap for Hyenacorvus]

[enter Vulpes Oscuria]

V. Oscuria: Murderer...

Hyenacorvus: Huh? What? Avast! Back, vixen! You shall not disturb him!

V. Oscuria: Why did you kill him?

Hyenacorvus: Because he asked such awful questions. Wait! No! I didn't kill him! He just has truth flu. He'll be ok. Maybe

V. Oscuria: Truth flu? It sounds dangerous. Why did you give it to him?

Hyenacorvus: I dunno. Do you know?

V. Oscuria: I suppose that's reason enough

S. Disrexus: Oohhhhh... what's this horriblis?

Hyenacorvus: The truth killed you but you're ok now

lxiv

S. Disrexus: How are you?

Pteracrotales: This warning is for you — things are not as they appear. You have been deceived, especially by yourself. Trust not your own knowledge. Trust not the knowledge of others. The belief that you understand leads to suffering at best, evil at worst. You will not escape this dilemma. You cannot think your way out of it. You might unthink your way out, but the process will likely kill you. Should you survive, madness will stalk you from all directions

S. Disrexus: That's nice. Should I believe you today?

[pause; her smile is worse than her glare]

Pteracrotales: There is a cure...

lxv

Hyenacorvus: Why are you doing that?

S. Disrexus: You mean resting?

Hyenacorvus: Whatever. Knock knock

S. Disrexus: Who's there?

Hyenacorvus: Cows go

S. Disrexus: Cows go who?

Hyenacorvus: No they don't! Cows are not owls! Anyway, knock knock

S. Disrexus: Who's there?

Hyenacorvus: I am

S. Disrexus: I am who?

Hyenacorvus: You don't know who you are? That's weird

S. Disrexus: It's common, actually

Hyenacorvus: To seek wisdom without losing our sacred wildness – for wisdom at the other's expense is costly and small. It is pretense only

Have you seen the reflection of a star on water? That is trading wildness for so-called wisdom. How can we be so deeply mistaken?

Chaos and order are inseparable. Whatever order we perceive is wrapped in chaos. Chaos partakes of an order too deep and wide for us to comprehend

S. Disrexus: That is mystic and heart-stirring

Hyenacorvus: Huh?

S. Disrexus: What you just said

Hyenacorvus: I was talking about chocolate, right?

S. Disrexus: No. You spoke of deep wisdom, order and

chaos. Say it again. I want to hear it again

Hyenacorvus: I'm pretty sure I was talking about chocolate

S. Disrexus: Fie!

Hyenacorvus: Do you have any chocolate? I would like some

[pause]

S. Disrexus: Sure, here you go

[time slows just a little]

Hyenacorvus: This is a good day

lxvi

V. Oscuria: Are you ready?

S. Disrexus: Yes

V. Oscuria: Liar. But it was my fault for asking

[sunset]

lxs

V. Fatalux: You're hurt

S. Disrexus: Not much

V. Fatalux: You're still bleeding

S. Disrexus: Looks worse than it is

V. Fatalux: Good enough then. Martini?

S. Disrexus: Sounds delicious

[dusk. bats fly overhead]

S. Disrexus: Nothing like a good martini. Thank you, friend

V. Fatalux: Happy to oblige. Survival is its own reward too, you know. Mostly

S. Disrexus: That it is

V. Fatalux: I'm sure you'll stop bleeding soon

[noctis]

FINIS

MORE

Mark writes at www.smilodondisrexus.org

Also: www.markmduncan.com